A Dreadful Murder

Minette Walters is a bestselling crime writer. She has written 12 novels and has won the CWA John Creasey Award, the Edgar Allan Poe Award and two CWA Gold Daggers for Fiction. *A Dreadful Murder* is her second Quick Read, following *Chickenfeed,* which was voted the 2006 Quick Reads Readers' Favourite. Minette Walters lives in Dorset with her husband.

Also by Minette Walters

The Ice House

The Sculptress

The Scold's Bridle

The Dark Room

The Echo

The Breaker

The Shape of Snakes

Acid Row

Fox Evil

Disordered Minds

The Tinder Box

The Devil's Feather

Chickenfeed
(a Quick Read)

The Chameleon's Shadow

Praise for Minette Walters

THE ICE HOUSE
'Terrific first novel with a high
Rendellesque frisson count'
The Times

THE SCULPTRESS
'A devastatingly effective novel'
Observer

THE SCOLD'S BRIDLE
'A gothic puzzle of great intricacy
and psychological power'
Sunday Times

THE DARK ROOM
'A marvellous, dramatically intelligent
novel. It shimmers with suspense, ambiguity
and a deep unholy joy'
Daily Mail

FOX EVIL
'*Fox Evil* is the work of a writer
at the peak of her confidence and
supreme ability'
The Times

DISORDERED MINDS
'A powerful, acute and vivid work from
a staggeringly talented writer'
Observer

THE TINDER BOX
'If there wasn't a recognised school
of crime writing called Home Counties
noir before, there is now. Minette Walters
invented it and remains the
undisputed Head Girl'
Birmingham Post

THE DEVIL'S FEATHER
'One of the most powerful yet nuanced
practitioners of the psychological thriller
... always keeps the narrative momentum
cracked up to a fierce degree'
Daily Express

A
Dreadful
Murder

Minette Walters

PAN BOOKS

First published 2013 by Pan Books
an imprint of Pan Macmillan, a division of Macmillan Publishers Limited
Pan Macmillan, 20 New Wharf Road, London N1 9RR
Basingstoke and Oxford
Associated companies throughout the world
www.panmacmillan.com

ISBN 978-1-4472-1323-9

1 3 5 7 9 8 6 4 2

A CIP catalogue record for this book is
available from the British Library.

Printed and bound by CPI Group (UK) Ltd, Croydon, CR0 4YY

Visit **www.panmacmillan.com** to read more about all our books
and to buy them. You will also find features, author interviews and
news of any author events, and you can sign up for e-newsletters
so that you're always first to hear about our new releases.

For Martin and Hannah Jones,
whose generous donation to Julia's House,
a children's hospice, has helped give
support and hope to families in Dorset.

Foreword

A *Dreadful Murder* is based on the true story of the shooting of Mrs Caroline Luard, which took place near the small village of Ightham* in Kent, on 24 August 1908. It remains one of the great unsolved mysteries of the twentieth century.

Mrs Luard was shot in broad daylight in the grounds of a large country estate called Frankfield House. She was nearly sixty years old, came from a wealthy, upper-class family, and was known in Ightham* for her charity work with the poor.

Her husband, Major-General Charles Luard, was a County Councillor and a Justice of the Peace. His closest friends were the Chief

* Pronounced **Item**

xi

Constable of Kent and the local MP. He was nearly seventy at the time of his wife's death.

Although no one was ever arrested for the crime, it was believed by many that Charles Luard murdered his wife in cold blood, and that his friends helped him escape justice.

Chapter One

Monday, 24 August 1908 –
Frankfield Park, afternoon

There was nothing in the clear blue skies over Kent to warn Caroline Luard she was about to die. The rain clouds had gone. The sun was shining. Everything was right with her world.

Or so it seemed.

She strolled with her husband, Charles, a retired Major-General, along the dusty lane that ran beside the dense woodland of Frankfield Park. Their fox terrier, Sergeant, loped ahead of them, tail wagging at every scent.

Perhaps they were talking about the holiday they were due to take in two days' time. Caroline was looking forward to the fresh sea air. Charles to some rounds of golf. Or perhaps, after thirty-three years of marriage, they had no need to speak at all.

Caroline had told her maid she would walk as far as the wicket gate into Frankfield Park. The Major-General would head on to Godden Green Golf Course to fetch his clubs. Caroline would return home through the woodland in time to greet a friend who was coming to tea.

The couple parted just beyond St Lawrence's Church. Charles's route would take him along the roads, Caroline's along a grassy footpath. Neither said goodbye. There was little point. They would see each other again in a couple of hours.

Even so, Caroline paused to watch as Charles strode down Church Road with their dog, Sergeant, beside him. The stoop of his shoulders made him look old. 'Try to get a lift home,' she called. 'You know how heavy your golf bag is. And don't forget Mrs Stewart is coming to tea. I'm sure she'd like to see you.'

Charles lifted a hand to show he'd heard, but he didn't turn round. Only Sergeant glanced back, ears pricked, for a last glimpse of his mistress.

* * *

Mary Stewart looked up in alarm as Major-General Luard swept into the drawing-room. She was twenty years younger than Charles and his brisk manner scared her.

'Where's Caroline?' he demanded.

Mary had been asking herself the same thing for twenty minutes. It made her uneasy to have been sitting in the Major-General's house without either of its owners present. 'I don't know,' she told him nervously. 'Your maid keeps telling me she'll be back any minute.'

Charles folded his tall frame into an armchair and stared at Mary. He looked puzzled. 'She started home two hours ago. I left her by the gate into Frankfield Park.'

'Perhaps she met someone along the way.' Mary tried a small smile. 'If it was Mrs Joliffe, it will be hours before she can get away.'

The old man gave a grunt of amusement, smoothing his long white moustache with a bony finger. 'Dreadful woman. Talks for England. Do you want some tea?'

He fired the words like pistol shots, and Mary looked guiltily at the teapot and cake stand which the maid had left on the low table in front of her. Was he expecting her to play hostess in Caroline's absence? 'Would *you* like some?' she asked.

Charles shook his head. 'Do you think she's had an accident? Fainted? Something like that?'

Mary gave a helpless shrug. 'Is that likely?'

'Don't imagine so. She's as fit as a fiddle.' He pushed himself to his feet again. 'Let's go and meet her. If she's with the Joliffe woman, she'll need rescuing.'

Mary followed him out of the house because she couldn't come up with a good reason not to. The Major-General wasn't the type to take no for an answer. He whistled up his dog, and they walked down the garden to the path that led through Frankfield Park.

Mary assumed Charles was matching his steps to hers out of politeness and urged him to go ahead at his own pace. 'I'll wait here for you.'

But he wasn't prepared to leave her behind. 'There's no hurry,' he said. 'Five minutes won't make a difference.'

Afterwards, when all the rumours started, this little episode set Mary thinking that the Major-General had wanted a witness when he found his wife. If so, she failed him. At five o'clock, she stopped at a path leading back to Ightham and said she had to go home.

'We have guests coming at six. Please tell Caroline I'll call on her tomorrow.'

Mary told her husband some days later that the Major-General looked annoyed when she said this, as if it wasn't part of his plan that she should leave. But Mr Stewart told her not to repeat the remark in public. There was too much gossip already and he didn't want his wife adding to it.

What people saw – and what they *thought* they saw – were rarely the same.

*   *   *

The first the outside world knew of Mrs Caroline Luard's brutal murder was when her husband ran from some woodland at the bottom of the long formal lawn in front of Frankfield House. Two gardeners – James Wickham and Walter Harding – heard his cries for help.

They hurried towards him but couldn't make out what he was saying. He was pointing towards an ornate summer house – known as La Casa – which stood amongst the trees. It was a single-storey building, surrounded by a raised wooden veranda and a picket fence. Very little of it was visible from the lawn.

'I thought the summer house must have fallen down,' James Wickham told the police later. 'But I couldn't see why that would put the Major-General into such a state.'

'He could hardly speak,' Walter Harding added. 'He was out of breath and weeping. He grabbed our sleeves and kept tugging us towards La Casa. I've never seen anyone so upset.'

The men were shocked at what they found. The body of a woman lay face down on the veranda. Her feet pointed towards the veranda gate as if she'd just mounted the steps, and her head was turned to the side with her left cheek uppermost. There was blood on her face, blood in her hair and vomit on the wooden boards. A few yards away was a straw hat with cherries on its brim and a cream silk glove turned inside-out.

'We could see she was dead,' Harding said. 'She looked so small . . . so shrunken. But we didn't realise it was Mrs Luard until the Major-General told us. It was just a bundle of clothes.'

Both men were moved by the old man's torment. He threw himself to his knees and clutched at the woman's hand. 'My darling wife,' he cried, tears falling freely down his face. 'My darling wife. She's gone . . . she's gone. I don't know what to do.'

James Wickham, the older gardener, reached down to help the Major-General to his feet. 'Best to step away, sir. There's nothing to be done for the lady now. By the looks of it, she's been shot. I'll take you up to the house while young Walter here goes for the police.'

No one was ever able to persuade Wickham or Harding that Charles Luard's distress wasn't real. They always insisted it was 'terrible to behold'. They knew the Major-General as a tall, imposing man with an air of command.

They didn't recognise him in the 'poor, sad person' who wept over the body of his wife.

But, once the tittle-tattle started, very few people were willing to believe them. Even a cold and distant man like the Major-General could summon up a show of grief if it meant he might avoid the hangman's noose. There was only one person likely to fire bullets into Mrs Luard's brain, and that was the stiff-necked old brute she'd married.

Chapter Two

Monday, 24 August 1908 –
Frankfield Park, late evening

With night falling, Henry Warde, the Chief Constable of Kent Police, ordered his men to light lanterns around the summer house. The soft yellow glow lent a strange beauty to the scene, though no one there could see it. They all agreed with their boss. This was an ugly business.

Dr John Mansfield, the local police surgeon, began by parting the blood-stained hair on the back of Caroline's head. 'Bullet wound,' he said, before leaning over to study the hole in her left cheek. 'It looks as if she was shot twice. First behind the right ear, then here, above the jaw.'

'What caused her to vomit?' Warde asked.

'Shock?' Dr Mansfield suggested, feeling the skin at the back of her skull. 'There's a large swelling here. I'm guessing she was hit with something hard – possibly a pistol or rifle butt – which knocked her to the ground. The shooting happened afterwards.'

'How long afterwards?'

'I can't say.' He pinched one of Caroline's hands to see if there was any sign of her body stiffening – the start of rigor mortis. 'It depends if the blow knocked her out. It may be that she was stunned for several minutes and vomited when she started to come round. Nausea is a common side effect of head injury. That may be the reason she was killed.'

'Explain.'

The doctor pushed himself to his feet and leaned on the picket fence. 'Perhaps the aim was never to kill her . . . only to knock her out and rob her. You say her purse and rings are missing. Her attacker may only have shot her because she opened her eyes and saw him.'

The Chief Constable walked a few steps to the nearest corner of the summer house. 'She'd have seen him anyway. Where could he have hidden? The door was locked. He had to be somewhere outside.'

'Or following her. The blow to the head was from behind.'

'Mm.' Warde tapped his walking stick on the veranda floor. 'You think it was a stranger? Someone who saw her in the woods and thought she might have some money on her?'

'It's possible.'

'But not very likely,' said Warde. 'A man would have to be very foolish to think a woman on a country stroll had large amounts of cash in her pocket. It doesn't happen.'

'What about her rings?'

Warde lifted his cane to point at the silk glove near Caroline's hat. 'Hidden under that. A casual thief wouldn't know she was wearing them until he peeled it off her hand. Why gamble on the gallows for money and rings that might not exist?'

Dr Mansfield shrugged. 'A twenty-year-old was hanged last month for killing a man for less than a pound. Do you think a passing tramp, acting on impulse, would use logic before he struck?'

The Chief Constable glanced at one of his inspectors, who was standing on the other side of the body. 'What do you say, George?'

George Hamble frowned. 'I can't see it being a vagrant, sir. Guns aren't cheap. If a man was that hard up, he'd have taken the weapon to a pawnbroker's instead of hanging around a deserted wood waiting for someone to pass.'

'Perhaps she disturbed him breaking into the building.'

'There's no sign of forced entry. But let's say you're right . . . Why shoot her? Why not jump the rail and run away? If we caught him later, the only thing we could arrest him for was trespass.'

'What other explanation is there?'

'Mrs Luard's rings and purse were stolen to make it look as if theft was the motive.'

'Meaning what?'

'Someone wanted her dead.' The Inspector stared down at the body. 'This looks more like an execution to me. A bang on the skull to bring her down then two shots to the brain. Did anyone other than her husband know she'd be here this afternoon?'

There was a short unhappy silence before Warde shook his head. 'If you're suggesting Charles killed his wife, I won't accept it, George. He's a close friend of mine. I've known him for years.'

The Inspector was well aware of the bond between his boss and the Major-General. 'Even so, we can't ignore him as a suspect, sir. In cases like this, it's always the husband we look at first.'

'But the man's in pieces. He's aged ten years in a matter of hours. There's no way he could have done this.'

Dr Mansfield stirred. 'Perhaps Mrs Luard asked someone to meet her.'

But the Chief Constable didn't like that idea either. 'Are you saying she had a secret meeting that her husband knew nothing about?' he demanded. 'I've never heard anything so absurd. They've been married for over thirty years.'

Mansfield smiled in spite of himself. 'I was just pointing out that there is more than one answer to the Inspector's question.' He levered himself off the picket fence and stretched to his full height. 'Can I leave you to remove the body? I'll do a full post-mortem tomorrow when I've had some sleep.'

Warde nodded.

'Will you take it amiss if I make another suggestion?' the doctor added.

'It depends what it is.'

'Call in Scotland Yard to run this inquiry, Henry. Most of your men respect and admire the Major-General . . . if only because he's a Justice of the Peace. It won't do him any good if the Kent Police Force is accused of turning a blind eye to evidence that might link him to the crime.'

The Chief Constable gave a long sigh. 'No,' he agreed. 'It's a rotten situation whichever way you look at it.'

*   *   *

Charles Luard's written record of where he was and what he did between 1.00 p.m. and 5.35 p.m. on Monday, 24 August 1908 – made at the request of his friend, Henry Warde:

Caroline and I sat down to lunch at one o'clock. We had cold mutton, followed by rhubarb flan and custard. I told her I needed to collect my golf clubs from Godden Green. She said she would come as far as the gate into Frankfield Park then take the footpath home.

We left the house shortly after two with Sergeant, our fox terrier. I remember Harriet, our parlourmaid, handing my wife her gloves and hat. She asked Caroline what time she expected to be back. Caroline said half past three. She also asked Harriet to remind Cook to warm the scones in the oven when Mrs Stewart arrived.

The afternoon was sunny, and Caroline and I did not walk fast. We separated at the wicket gate into Frankfield Park. The time was half past two. Caroline urged me to try for a lift home because my golf bag is heavy. She was always concerned that the weight would damage my back. That was the last time we spoke to each other.

Sergeant and I continued along Church Road then branched off towards Godden Green. I reached the Clubhouse some time between half past three and a quarter to four.

I did not see anyone I knew. I collected my bag from my locker and left again for home.

Sergeant and I stayed on the main road in the hope of being offered a lift. Shortly after four o'clock, the vicar came towards us in his motor car. He was going the wrong way but he stopped for a quick chat. He explained that he had an errand to perform but agreed to pick us up on his way back.

He urged me to put my bag in his car to save me the trouble of carrying it any further. If his errand took longer than expected, he would bring the clubs to my house. However, he returned at about twenty past four and dropped Sergeant and me at Ightham Knoll* some five to ten minutes later.

Harriet, the maid, informed me that Mrs Stewart had arrived but that Caroline had not returned. I joined Mrs Stewart in the drawing-room and we spoke for several minutes. I was concerned that Caroline might have had a fall and suggested we set out to meet her. Mrs Stewart agreed.

* Pronounced **Item Noll**

We walked down the garden and took the footpath towards Frankfield Park. There was no sign of Caroline anywhere. Mrs Stewart said she had to leave because she had guests coming. I continued alone along the path.

By then I was becoming very anxious. It was well after five o'clock and I had parted from Caroline some two and a half hours earlier. If she had tripped or fallen, she had been lying untended for a long time.

I saw her as soon as I reached the clearing around the summer house. She was lying on the veranda and I rushed forward to help her. It did not occur to me that she had been shot. I assumed she had fainted or suffered some kind of stroke. When I drew closer, I saw the pallor of her face, the blood in her hair and on her cheek.

I rocked her shoulder but it was clear to me she was dead. There is no mistaking when the soul has gone. I have lived too long and seen too many soldiers die in battle.

The shock was terrible. I had no idea what to do. In all my years, I have never had to deal with such grief as I felt. I remember running towards Frankfield House, calling out for someone to help me. I have since been told that this happened at around half past five.

I believe my wife was killed for her rings. There is no other explanation that makes sense. I am as sure as I can be that Caroline did not have an enemy in the world. She was loved and admired by everyone who knew her.

The Kent Messenger – *early edition, Tuesday, 25 August 1908:*

A Dreadful Murder at Frankfield Park

The body of a lady was discovered yesterday on premises owned by Mr & Mrs Wilkinson of Frankfield House. Mystery surrounds the death but our reporter has learnt that the victim was Mrs Caroline Luard of Ightham. Her husband Major-General Charles Luard is a leading citizen of Kent. Scotland Yard has been called in to conduct the inquiry.

It is believed that Mrs Luard was shot during a robbery. Her purse and rings were stolen and the police are searching the county for armed vagrants.

Chapter Three

Tuesday, 25 August 1908 –
Sevenoaks, morning

Henry Warde met the two Scotland Yard detectives, Superintendent Albert Taylor and Constable Harold Philpott, off the train. The constable was dressed in the uniform of the London police but the Superintendent wore a brown overcoat over a dark suit.

Superintendent Taylor was a tall, good-looking, middle-aged man, who had an easy way of inspiring confidence in the people he met. He removed his soft felt hat and shook the Chief Constable's hand. 'Good day, sir.'

Warde had spoken to him on the telephone earlier that morning but he still felt the need to explain why he'd asked for Scotland Yard's help. 'I can't be seen to take sides,' he said, leading the two men towards his car. 'I knew the dead woman well. Her husband's a close friend.'

Taylor nodded. 'You told me you didn't think the Major-General was involved. Have your men found anything to change that view?'

'No,' said Warde. 'His own account of what he did during the time she was killed has been backed up by four witnesses who saw him.' He drew to a halt beside his Daimler and took two pieces of paper from his pocket. 'This is Charles's account . . . and this is what the witnesses have told us.'

The Superintendent scanned the first page before handing it to Constable Philpott. He then read the second page.

3.20 p.m. Thomas Durrand of Hall Farm saw Major-General Luard pass the farm entrance.

3.30 p.m. Peter Filey, labourer, saw Major-General Luard near Godden Green Golf Course.

3.35 p.m. The Club steward saw Major-General Luard walking up the grounds.

4.05 p.m. Reverend A. B. Cotton passed Major-General Luard in his car. He stopped and put Luard's golf clubs in his vehicle.

4.20 p.m. Reverend Cotton gave the Major-General and his dog a lift home.

'How far is it from where Luard left his wife at the wicket gate to this first sighting at Hall Farm?' Taylor asked, placing his finger on the first line. 'There's a gap of fifty minutes . . . assuming he's telling the truth about parting from her at half past two.'

'A fair distance. I'd say fifty minutes is about right for a man of Charles's age. He's almost seventy.'

'And there's no question the couple left the house just after two?'

'The maid confirmed it.'

'Could the Major-General have reached Hall Farm by 3.20 if he'd followed his wife to the summer house first?'

Warde shook his head. 'Not on foot . . . on a bicycle, possibly.'

'With a dog racing along beside him,' Taylor murmured thoughtfully. 'That's the bit that interests me. In some ways, Sergeant is his best alibi.'

'Why?'

'There's no saying how an animal will behave. Sergeant might have tried to protect his mistress . . . become excited by the blood . . . started howling . . . refused to leave the body. Any or all of those would have caused problems. If the Major-General's guilty, he took a big risk on the dog.'

'And on anyone seeing him,' Warde pointed out. 'It was pure chance that Thomas Durrand happened to be at his farm entrance. Dog or not, it was a damn strange way to kill a wife if he wanted to get away with it. What sort of murderer admits to being the last person to see his victim alive and the first to find her dead?'

'An idiot or a genius,' Taylor said. 'The simpler the story, the harder it is to disprove.'

*　　*　　*

Warde drove the two detectives to the mortuary, a small brick building next to the hospital in Sevenoaks. They found Dr Mansfield at work on the post-mortem. The three men joined him and stared gravely at Caroline Luard's corpse.

For the sake of decency, John Mansfield had covered her body with a white sheet. He folded the cloth back to the neck to reveal Caroline's head. 'I've shaved the hair around the wounds,' he said. 'You can clearly see the bruise where she was struck with something heavy . . . and the bullet holes behind her right ear and in her cheek. I'm going to have to make a mess of her if you want me to dig them out.'

'It has to be done,' Taylor said with regret. 'We need to know what sort of weapon was used.'

Warde looked doubtful. 'Can you tell that from a fired bullet?' he asked.

'Not personally, but I know someone who can.' Taylor took a notebook and pencil from his pocket. 'Edwin Churchill. We've used him several times. He has a gunsmith business in The Strand . . . knows more about the science of shooting than any man I know. He calls it "ballistics".'

'How do we get hold of him?'

'By telegram.' The Superintendent scribbled a couple of lines and tore off the page. 'How close is the nearest post office?' he asked the doctor.

'Two hundred yards up the road.'

Taylor handed the note to his constable. 'Sign it from me and wait for an answer. If Churchill can come this afternoon, telegraph back to say we'll meet him at the station. When we're finished here, we'll pick you up from the post office.'

'Will do, sir.'

Taylor waited until the door closed then moved to the top of the table. He stooped to look at the darkened bruise on Caroline's scalp. 'How long does it take for something like this to develop, Doctor?'

'Long enough for the broken veins to leak blood and fluid into the skin.'

'But only if the victim's alive?'

'Indeed. The heart has to keep pumping to make a bruise as obvious as this one.'

'So what's your best guess on the time lag between the bang on the head and the first shot?'

Dr Mansfield shrugged. 'A few minutes. To be honest, I'm more interested in why she was sick on the floor of the veranda. It's possible she vomited from the shock of being struck . . . but I think it more likely she was knocked out and was sick when she started to come round.'

The doctor explained what he thought had been the sequence of events. Since Caroline had been hit from behind, she would have fallen forwards. If she was shocked but still awake, she would have thrust out her hands to break her fall. If she was knocked right out, she'd have collapsed in one movement.

'It makes more sense that she went down in one movement,' he said. 'We wouldn't have found the vomit where we did if she fell to her hands and knees first.'

'No,' said Taylor, picturing the scene in his mind. 'It would have been underneath her. Her body would have covered it when she was shot.'

'That's my guess.'

'And if she had been knocked out for several minutes, it would explain why the bruise had time to develop.'

'Indeed.' Mansfield paused. 'The pity is she didn't remain unconscious. She might still be alive if she hadn't come round.'

The Superintendent from Scotland Yard was a lot sharper than Kent's Chief Constable. It took him only a matter of seconds to follow the logic of what the doctor was saying. 'You think that's why she's dead? She opened her eyes and saw her killer?'

Mansfield nodded. 'She'd have been able to describe him . . . might even have known him by name.'

* * *

Henry Warde picked holes in the doctor's ideas while he and Taylor sat in the Daimler, waiting for Constable Philpott to finish in the post office. There was no evidence that Caroline ever opened her eyes again, he argued. It was just as likely she was clubbed down and shot immediately.

Taylor listened to him while watching the people of Sevenoaks pass by. They seemed to have more time to pause and greet their friends than their fellows on the crowded streets of London. Signs of wealth were everywhere – in the buildings, in the number of cars on the road and in the clothes on display.

'You're reading too much into the doctor's words,' the Superintendent murmured when Warde fell silent. 'He didn't say she recognised her husband when she opened her eyes.'

The Chief Constable sighed. 'Maybe not, but that's what people will think. Charles is a crack shot, and everyone knows it. He founded the Rifle Club to teach every working man how to handle a gun in the event of war. He could have killed Caroline from a hundred yards away.'

'In which case, she wouldn't have the bang on her head,' Taylor reminded him. 'Any Tom, Dick or Harry can shoot straight when he's right up close.'

'It won't stop the gossip. As one of my inspectors said last night, a dead wife usually means a guilty husband.'

'Does the Major-General have money

worries? It's when the debts start to pile up that wives become a burden.'

'I wouldn't know,' said Warde. 'He's a proud man. He'd never admit to his friends that he couldn't pay his bills. But I can't see it. Caroline ran charities for the poor, and she used her own and Charles's money to support them.'

'What about another woman?' Taylor asked, watching a pretty girl swing her long skirts from side to side as she flirted with a lad. 'That's always a good reason to get rid of a wife.'

Warde followed his gaze. 'I'd be surprised,' was all he said.

Chapter Four

Constable Philpott rejoined them with news that the gun expert would be catching the five o'clock train. Chief Constable Warde suggested they visit Charles Luard next but London's Superintendent Taylor shook his head. He needed to get a 'feel' for where the crime took place before he spoke to the victim's husband. He also wanted to see the wicket gate into Frankfield Park and follow the route the Major-General said he had taken to Godden Green Golf Club.

The boss from Scotland Yard ruled out walking the footpath to the summer house. On orders from *his* bosses in London, Taylor had sent for bloodhounds to sniff out the escape route that Mrs Luard's killer might have taken. But he had few hopes the dogs would succeed.

With only the scents from the veranda to go by, the chances were high that the animals would simply retrace Caroline's tracks back to the road.

Chief Constable Warde headed his Daimler in the direction of Ightham, turning off onto Church Road before they reached the village. He paused briefly beside the wicket gate then drove to Godden Green, passing Hall Farm on the way.

'It's a long walk for a seventy-year-old,' Taylor said. 'Was he really planning to make the return trip with a golf bag on his shoulder?'

'He'd have had no choice if the vicar hadn't given him a lift.' Warde stopped the Daimler at the side of the golf course. 'He still had to walk across these grounds to the Clubhouse . . . and that's no mean distance either.'

'He must be a fitter man than I am.'

'You'll have to add another couple of miles if he followed Caroline to the summer house. He'd have been running most of the way.'

'It doesn't seem likely,' Taylor agreed.

'You'll doubt it even more when you meet him,' Warde said. 'I've never seen a man so broken by his wife's death.'

The Superintendent eyed him for a moment. 'Perhaps it was the way she was killed that upset him,' he said. 'Perhaps he hadn't expected it to be so brutal.'

'Meaning what?'

'He may have hired someone to do it for him while he created an excuse, an alibi, for himself.'

'Is that a serious suggestion?'

Taylor shrugged. 'He was the only one other than Mrs Luard who knew where she'd be yesterday afternoon.'

* * *

The three policemen reached the summer house by driving to Frankfield House and walking down the long lawn to the woodland at the bottom of the garden. Warde pointed out where the gardeners, James Wickham and Walter Harding, had been working when Charles had burst from the trees calling for help.

If the truth be told, Taylor was a little offended by the size of the summer house,

La Casa. It was large enough to house four or five families in the poorer parts of London. He viewed it as a rich man's plaything.

Two Kent policemen stood on guard in front of it. They were there to prevent the curious gawping at where murder had been done. They saluted smartly as the Chief Constable and the Scotland Yard detectives approached.

'Any trouble?' Warde asked.

'We've turned a few visitors away, sir. It's the blood they want to see.'

'Just morbid folk,' said Warde with a grunt of disgust. 'Did you take their names?'

'I've made a list. They were mostly youngsters from Ightham. I'll have words with their parents later.'

'Have the dogs arrived?' Taylor asked.

'About an hour ago, sir. They headed off in that direction.' The man pointed towards the path leading to Church Road. 'I told their handler it was the way Mrs Luard must have come, and he said it was probably her scent they were following.'

Taylor nodded. 'It was always going to be a long shot. At least we're free to go where we like now.' He pointed to the gate in the veranda fence. 'Is that where Mrs Luard entered?'

'Must have been,' Warde said. 'It's the only way in.' He led the detectives across the grass. 'You can see where she was lying. She hadn't even reached the door before she was hit.'

Taylor examined the ground in front of the steps. 'The earth's quite soft. Did you look for footprints?'

'Yes, but there were too many to pick out the culprit's. We found some of Caroline's smaller ones in places . . . but Charles, Wickham and Harding walked or ran over this patch several times. Some of my men crossed it too.'

'What about the paths?'

'Same problem. They've taken a lot of traffic. The doctor and I came from Church Road, and Inspector Hamble brought his team from Ightham.'

Taylor walked a good twenty yards in the direction Caroline had come from. If she'd been running away from a pursuer, her prints would have been far apart and her heels would have dug into the ground. He found one or two indentations in the grass that were small enough to be made by a woman, but nothing to indicate a frightened run.

He returned to Warde. 'How did you remove the body?'

'By stretcher to Ightham Knoll. I called for an ambulance from there to take it to Sevenoaks.'

'Ightham Knoll being Mrs Luard's home?'

'Yes. It seemed better than causing a stir amongst the staff in Frankfield House. We were able to take her straight upstairs to her bedroom.'

'Did the Major-General spend any time with her alone?'

'No. He and I sat in the drawing-room until the transport arrived. I urged him to write that account you've read. He made his goodbyes to her when she left.'

Inwardly, Taylor was cursing the Chief Constable for waiting twelve hours to call him. Scotland Yard had modern views about how to conduct a murder inquiry, and they did not include trampling the ground around a murder scene or taking the victim back to her own house.

Taylor, now a Scotland Yard Superintendent,

had been a fresh-faced constable in 1888 when Jack the Ripper had prowled the streets of Whitechapel. And if that monster had taught the police anything, it was to be careful with the evidence. How much easier his job would be now, he thought, if Warde had had the sense to summon him before the body had been removed.

Instead, he had to rely on the other man's memory, and try to picture the scene for himself. 'How was she lying?'

'On her front. Her head was where the bloodstains are.'

'And which way was she facing?'

'Feet towards the gate . . . head towards the summer house door.'

Taylor mounted the steps and examined the stains on the wooden floor. 'There's not much blood. She must have died from the first shot. I wonder why the killer gambled on a second one.'

'How was it a gamble?'

'Noise,' said Taylor, glancing across the glade towards Frankfield House. 'He should have been afraid of being heard.' He stepped around the bloodstains to peer through one of the windows into the summer house. 'When do you think the rings were taken from Mrs Luard's fingers?'

'After she was dead?'

Taylor tested the door to see if it was locked. 'We're talking about a killer who'd just unleashed a couple of loud gunshots . . . had no idea if anyone had heard them . . . and chose to squat calmly in his victim's blood to wrestle a glove off her hand. Does that seem likely to you?'

'Not when you put it like that.'

'I'm guessing he ran like the devil in case his escape route was cut off.' Taylor took a last look at where Caroline had fallen. 'I think the doctor's right. She was knocked unconscious and the rings were taken before she was shot.'

Warde began to look more cheerful. 'If theft was the motive, we can rule out Charles.'

Taylor gave a regretful shake of his head. 'Not if it was part of his murder plan.' He stepped off the veranda. 'But why make her death so noisy? She was at her killer's mercy. He could have strangled her or beaten her to death.'

* * *

As Henry Warde drove towards Ightham, Taylor found himself more and more persuaded by Dr Mansfield's version of events. If the aim had been to murder the woman, why not grab her from behind and run a knife across her throat? As long as she died quietly, her killer had all the time in the world to take whatever he wanted.

And why two shots? Taylor thought of how bodies twitched and moved after they were dead, and wondered if panic had played a part. He could easily imagine the sudden flap of a hand spooking an already frightened man into shooting again. If so, the murder was the work of a novice rather than a hired killer or a retired soldier.

He spoke his next thoughts aloud. 'Whoever did it wasn't at work yesterday . . . unless the killer is one of the gardeners in Frankfield Park.'

'They operate in pairs and they've all been vouched for.' Warde shook his head. 'A jobless vagrant *has* to be the most likely suspect. Nothing else makes sense.'

Taylor watched through the windscreen of the car as some houses came into view. 'What sort of crimes do you have in Kent?' he asked.

'Pickpocketing . . . house burglary . . . minor thefts from shops . . . poaching. Nothing like Caroline's murder.'

'And you always know where to look for your thieves?'

Warde gave a grunt of amusement. 'We have our share of ne'er-do-wells if that's what you mean.'

Taylor gazed out of the window as the Daimler cruised down Ightham High Street. Medieval half-timbered houses lined the road and they looked as expensive as anything he'd seen in Sevenoaks. 'How many of your ne'er-do-wells live here?' he asked.

Warde's amusement grew. 'This isn't a London slum, Superintendent. It's one of the oldest and most desirable villages in Kent.'

Taylor smiled. 'On the surface,' he agreed, 'but there must be some desperate people here too.'

'What makes you say that?'

'Mrs Luard would have had nothing to fill her days if she hadn't had her charity work to keep her busy.'

Chapter Five

Henry Warde had described the Major-General as 'broken' by his wife's death and that was certainly how he seemed to Taylor. The custom of the times was that men controlled themselves. It was only women who wept for the people they loved. Yet tears were coursing freely down Charles Luard's cheeks.

Far from the fit old man who had walked five or six miles the day before, Taylor was faced with a frail shadow. The Major-General's hands shook with constant tremors and his face was drawn with grief.

They sat in the drawing-room at Ightham

Knoll. There were reminders of Mrs Luard everywhere. Her portrait as a young woman on the wall. Flowers on the table. Cushions, scented with lavender. Pretty china on the sideboard. Photographs.

Henry Warde clearly had no idea how to deal with his friend. He stood with his back to the room, staring out towards the garden. He muttered phrases like, 'Come on, old chap, a few deep breaths should do the trick.' Or, 'There's no point giving way like this. Nothing's going to bring her back.'

But Taylor took a different tack. Thicker-skinned than the Chief Constable – and not so convinced that the Major-General's grief was real – he parked himself on a chair and leaned forward, staring into the old man's face.

It wasn't long before Luard became uneasy and regained some control. 'What do you want to know?' he asked. 'I wrote an account for Henry last night.'

Taylor began with simple questions. How long had the Major-General and Mrs Luard been married? How long had they lived at

41

Ightham Knoll? Did they have children? Was Mrs Luard liked in the village?

He learnt that the couple had had two sons – both in the Army – but the younger had died on service in Africa in 1903. That Charles and Caroline had lived at Ightham Knoll for twenty years. That Caroline had a wide circle of friends and was known, and admired, for her kindness and her work with the poor.

In sudden despair, the Major-General placed his head in his hands. 'She never harmed anyone,' he cried. 'Who would want to kill her?'

'That's what we're here to find out, sir. From what you've said, she had no enemies in Ightham.'

'Or anywhere else. How could she? We spent our days together. There was nothing I didn't know about her life.'

Taylor doubted that. Most women kept secrets from their husbands, if only how much they paid for their hats. 'What about you, sir? Do you have any enemies?'

'Why do you ask?'

'Someone may have thought that killing Mrs Luard was an easier revenge than killing you.

A lady alone has no defence.' Taylor watched him for a moment. 'You're a Justice of the Peace. Have you ever received threats from men you've sent to prison?'

'Only in court. Most of them feel their sentences are unfair.' Charles raised his head, his face haggard with guilt. 'Are you saying this was my fault? Should I have warned her?'

'No, sir. I'm just running through possible motives.'

'Her rings and purse were stolen. Isn't that motive enough?'

'Perhaps,' Taylor agreed. 'But Dr Mansfield says she was stunned by a blow to the back of the head first. And a thief had no need to kill her if she was unable to fight back.'

Charles looked blank. 'The doctor must be wrong.'

'I'm afraid not, sir. He believes your wife was knocked out for several minutes before she was shot. We're guessing that's when her rings were taken . . . either because theft was the aim or because that's what the culprit wanted us to think.'

He was watching the Major-General's face

closely. If Luard had planned his wife's death, he was hoping to see a reaction: a flicker of alarm because the doctor and detectives were on the right track – or a flicker of relief because they weren't.

'You talk as if this man was sane,' Charles said, raising his hands in futile protest. 'But no sane person would have done this.'

'I wish I could agree with you. Sadly, in my job, you learn very quickly that sane men can be far more brutal than lunatics.'

The old man's eyes welled with tears. 'My wife wouldn't have refused him money, you know. She was a very Christian person. All he had to do was ask.'

'What if she knew he didn't deserve her help? The world is full of husbands who take every penny their wives receive to spend on drink. If he was a local man she might have come across him through her charity work. How would Mrs Luard have reacted if someone like that had asked her for money?'

For the first time, Taylor understood why Luard had risen to Major-General in the Army and why he was a Justice of the Peace. It was the not knowing that had left him bereft. Faced with a possible answer, his faded eyes came back to life.

'She'd have told him to go home and sober up,' he barked. 'She had no time for drunks who left their children to starve. Is that the kind of person you're looking for?'

'It's a possibility,' Taylor told him. 'Can you give us any names? Families your wife worked with?'

Luard shook his head. 'You'll have to ask her friends. They'll be able to give you a better list than I can. Caroline sits on a number of committees.' He realised he'd used the wrong tense. 'I can't believe she's dead,' he said sadly.

*   *   *

Mary Stewart lived in one of the half-timbered houses overlooking the village green in Ightham. She seemed to think that having three policemen in her house was a cause for alarm, and gave way to near faints every time Taylor asked her a question. He found her empty-headed and silly, and had trouble keeping his patience with her.

45

Most of what she told them related to her long wait in the drawing-room at Ightham Knoll before Charles arrived. Overnight, she had 'remembered' feelings of doom. 'I knew something terrible had happened,' she gasped, tapping her chest. 'I felt it here.'

'Then I'm surprised you helped the Major-General look for his wife,' Taylor said. 'Weren't you frightened of what you'd find?'

'*Dreadfully* frightened. I told him I couldn't go any further.'

'I thought you went home to meet some guests, Mrs Stewart?'

She fanned her face with her hand. 'I'd have gone anyway. Charles was being very strange.'

'How?'

'He kept slowing his pace so that I wouldn't lag behind. I think he wanted me there when he found her.'

'Meaning what? That he knew she was dead?'

The woman wriggled her shoulders. 'It was just very odd, that's all. I don't know Charles well enough to walk *any* distance with him.'

'Particularly if you had such strong feelings of doom,' Taylor murmured drily.

It wasn't just Taylor who thought her silly. Henry Warde's scornful clearing of his throat was so pointed that it set the woman blushing to the roots of her hair. It meant she took a dislike to him, and had fewer concerns later about joining in the gossip that the Chief Constable of Kent would do anything to protect his friend.

* * *

'Idiotic creature,' Henry Warde, the Chief Constable, said as he led the way back to his Daimler. 'She'll be saying she saw a gun in Charles's golf bag next.'

Taylor leaned on the roof of the car. 'Did you search it last night?'

'Matter of fact, I did. First thing I thought of after Hamble said the murder looked planned. I checked his rifles as well but none of them had been fired recently.'

'What about handguns?'

'Three revolvers. All clean. He said he couldn't remember if he had any bullets for them . . . or where they might be.' Warde glared

47

up at the Stewarts' house. 'It won't stop that silly woman inventing stories if it suits her.'

Taylor scanned the names that he'd finally prised out of Mary Stewart. They weren't the ones he'd wanted. She'd thrown a fainting fit when he suggested that Caroline might have come across her killer through her charity work. And rather than give him a list of suspects, she'd offered some worthy ladies who were 'bound' to know more than she did.

'Then let's hope Mrs Luard's other friends are more sensible,' he said, tucking the page into his coat pocket. 'We won't get very far if they all stay silent for fear of being killed themselves.'

*   *   *

The Kent Messenger – *late edition,*
Tuesday, 25 August 1908:

Brutal Slaying of a Kent Lady

The shooting of Mrs Caroline Luard has excited public concern. Law-abiding citizens are asking how a lady of Kent could have been murdered in broad daylight.

The mystery surrounding the death continues. Mrs Luard was taking an afternoon stroll through the woodland around Frank-field Park when she was attacked. But police are puzzled as to why a thief thought she had anything worth stealing.

While robbery still appears to be the most likely motive, a Kent detective has told our reporter that minds remain open on whether the murder was planned. Mrs Luard may have been followed or her killer may have known in advance which route she intended to take home.

An inquest will be heard tomorrow at Major-General Luard's house in Ightham.

Chapter Six

Warde checked his watch and offered the Scotland Yard detectives a pint of beer and a sandwich. They were standing outside Sevenoaks station and he pointed to the Farmer's Inn, which was across the road. 'It's as good a place as any,' he told them. 'They have rooms if you don't want to return to London tonight.'

All three men were tired. They had met the gunsmith – Edwin Churchill – off the five o'clock train and had spent the last two hours watching him study the used bullets recovered from Caroline Luard's brain. His methods were slow because he repeated every action several times. When he wasn't staring down the lens of his microscope, he was using pincers and tiny rulers on different parts of the crushed metal casings.

He also spent a long time looking at the wounds in Caroline Luard's skull. He pointed out flecks of soot on her skin, which had been caused by flames in the barrel of the gun when the bullets had been fired.

His conclusion – stated with absolute confidence – was that she had been shot by a .32 revolver at a distance of a few inches.

'The man clearly knows what he's talking about,' said Warde as he led Taylor and Philpott into the saloon bar.

Taylor pulled out a chair at an empty table and sat down. 'He claims it's only a matter of time before he'll be able to prove which guns fire which bullets. It seems barrels are like fingerprints. No two are the same.'

Warde lowered himself wearily onto another chair. 'It's a pity he can't do it now. It would help at the inquest if he could say that none of Charles's weapons were used.'

'It depends what calibre of bullets they fire. If the barrel widths are less than .32, they can certainly be ruled out.' Taylor broke off while a waitress took their order. 'Which doesn't mean there wasn't a fourth revolver that Luard hasn't told you about.'

The Chief Constable sighed. 'Do you still see him as a suspect?'

'Not at the moment.' Taylor took out a tobacco pouch and started to roll a cigarette. 'But my mind will change very quickly if we find any evidence that his marriage wasn't as perfect as he wants us to think.'

* * *

Seven miles away at the George & Dragon in Ightham, late editions of the local newspaper were being passed from hand to hand. No one was surprised that Kent police were keeping an open mind about Mrs Luard's murder.

Few of the regulars at the George & Dragon had any liking for Major-General Luard. One or two had been on the receiving end of his over-lengthy sentences and the rest resented his high-handed manner. They saw him as a cold and distant man who thought the working classes beneath him.

In any case, it was well known that Mrs

Luard was a deeply unhappy woman. For no reason at all, she would burst into tears in front of friends and strangers. It was well known, too, that the Major-General used golf as an excuse to leave home every Tuesday and Thursday in order to visit the house of a certain lady in the village.

The dissenting voices of the gardeners, James Wickham and Walter Harding, were drowned out. No one believed that a controlled and rigid man like the Major-General would weep openly over his dead wife and call her 'his darling'.

The truth was more simple. The pub customers thought Mrs Luard had found out about her husband's affair, and the Major-General – bored with her complaints, or scared by her threats of divorce for adultery – had shot her.

*   *   *

The inquest was held the next morning in the drawing-room at Ightham Knoll. Such was the interest of the locals that there was standing room only by the time Taylor, Philpott and the gunsmith, Edwin Churchill, entered the room.

They had arrived an hour before so that Churchill, who'd caught an early train, could examine the Major-General's weapons and ammunition. But they hadn't reckoned on so many people wanting to hear the gory details of Mrs Luard's death.

Taylor wondered if Henry Warde had been wise to choose this room for the event. As Dr Mansfield gave his post-mortem report, all eyes were on the portrait of Caroline as a beautiful and vibrant young woman. It was hard to remember that she was fifty-eight at the time of her death and had been married for thirty-three years to the elderly man who made his statement after the doctor.

A whispered comment floated back to Taylor. 'What's the betting it was *her* who was having the affair?'

The Major-General did himself no favours by the clipped way he gave his evidence. To Taylor it was clear that he was trying to keep his emotions in check, but it made him seem uncaring about the fate of his wife. There was very little sympathy for him in the room.

Indeed, one or two spectators protested loudly that the inquest was being bent in his favour. Why had the Coroner allowed it to be held in the Major-General's own home? And why was his close friend, the Chief Constable of Kent, in charge of the inquiry?

From the remarks being made, there seemed to be a genuine belief in the room that Charles Luard was guilty. Yet Taylor didn't understand why, since most of the evidence pointed to someone else being the murderer.

Henry Warde's men had found two members of staff at Frankfield House – Daniel Kettle and Anna Wickham – who said they'd heard gunshots at 3.15 on the afternoon of Monday, 24 August. Since Thomas Durrand saw Charles Luard pass Hall Farm at 3.20 – a fifty-minute walk away – the Coroner made the point that it couldn't have been the Major-General who fired the shots.

When Edwin Churchill gave his evidence, he produced a careful summary of the type of weapon and size of bullets that had been used to kill Mrs Luard. He also displayed the Major-General's three revolvers and used a .32 bullet to show the barrels were too narrow to take it.

Taylor's own evidence was brief. He had taken charge of Mrs Luard's clothes following the post-mortem, and he described how the pocket in her dress had been ripped. The Coroner asked him if he had any idea why that should be so.

'I'm told she carried her purse in it. I assume the killer tore the pocket in his haste to get at the money.'

'Do you have any doubt that theft was the motive?'

But Taylor wasn't prepared to put his cards on the table at that time. 'We are looking at everything,' he said.

* * *

'You should have come down on the side of armed robbery,' Henry Warde grumbled after the inquest was halted. 'Now we have to go through the whole thing again because that silly fool of a Coroner was too afraid to rule she was murdered by someone unknown.'

They were standing by the Daimler, waiting for Constable Philpott to bring Churchill outside. 'Do you blame the Coroner?' Taylor asked. 'If he'd given in to the hostility in that room, he'd have named the Major-General as Mrs Luard's killer.'*

'He'd have listened to a Scotland Yard detective,' Warde said irritably.

Taylor gave an amused laugh. 'You think so? I got the feeling no one was being heard. Besides, I didn't want to reveal too much to the newspapers. I saw a couple of reporters from the London rags in there.'

'They'll write what they like anyway.'

'Indeed, but we've a better chance of finding Mrs Luard's rings if the culprit thinks we suspect the Major-General.'

*In 1908 a Coroner could name a suspect in a murder case if he felt the evidence was strong enough. But such verdicts, made under pressure from the public, were often wrong. Today, it is the job of the police to decide if and when to release the names of suspects.

'You're hoping he'll pawn them?'

'If he's stupid, he will. If he's not. . . he'll have tossed them into the nearest river.'

* * *

Unsigned letter addressed to Major-General Luard, Ightham, Kent – received by the evening post on Wednesday, 26 August 1908:

WE ALL KNOW YOU SHOT YOUR WIFE.

YOUR FRIEND THE CHIEF CONSTABLE CAN'T PROTECT YOU FOREVER.

YOU DON'T DESERVE TO LIVE.

DO EVERYONE A FAVOUR.

KILL YOURSELF.

Chapter Seven

Despite all their efforts in the days following Caroline Luard's murder, the police made little progress in finding her killer.

Henry Warde, the Chief Constable of Kent, took the lead in searching the county for armed vagrants and men sentenced by Major-General Luard in his role as Justice of the Peace. The Chief Constable also dispatched teams to check the pawn shops and go house-to-house seeking anyone who had seen strangers in and around Frankfield Park on the day of the crime.

Inspector George Hamble was tasked with taking a close look at the Major-General's story. It seemed even more solid after a couple of woodcutters came forward to say that they too had heard gunshots in Frankfield Park at 3.15. But Henry Warde wanted every aspect of his friend's alibi checked in order to clear him.

What was the shortest time that Charles and Caroline could have walked to the summer house from their home, Ightham Knoll? Was there a shortcut that Charles could have taken from the summer house to Hall Farm? Was there any evidence he'd recently bought or borrowed a revolver? Or had contact with a hired assassin?

After days of work, all Hamble was able to say was that no one, however fit, could have reached Hall Farm by 3.20 if the shooting happened at 3.15. He had looked at the possibility that the witnesses had heard different gunfire – someone out game hunting perhaps – but the timings didn't work for that either.

'At a very fast walk, the Luards could have reached the summer house by 2.30,' he told the Chief Constable. 'And if Mrs Luard had died then, the Major-General could have run to Hall Farm by 3.20, but—' he broke off.

'But what?'

'I can't see why his wife would agree to it. She knew the Major-General's plan was to go to Godden Green for his golf clubs because the housemaid heard them discussing it over lunch. What reason could he have come up with for taking her at a fast trot to the summer house first?'

The Inspector had had no better luck trying to unearth whether the Major-General had purchased a revolver or dealt with a killer. 'I can't be certain that neither of those things happened,' he went on, 'but none of the Major-General's staff believes he wanted his wife dead. One of the maids, Jane Pugmore, told me she never heard a cross word between them in the six years she's worked at their house.'

'What about these rumours that Caroline was unhappy?'

'It depends who you listen to. According to Jane, Mrs Luard shed tears whenever she was reminded of her son. He died abroad and she never had a chance to comfort him.'

'What do other people say?'

'That her husband was having an affair with a woman in the village.' Hamble shrugged at the other man's frown. 'No one's been able to name her . . . It's just gossip from the grapevine.

I'm beginning to feel quite sorry for the Major-General. They all want to see him hanged.'

'But why do they hate him so much?' Warde asked, staring gloomily at his hands. 'Has anyone given a reason for it?'

Hamble shook his head. 'Not really. It seems to be driven by those at the bottom. They say Mrs Luard passed the time of day with them but the Major-General doesn't bother.'

Taylor had focused on the motive for the murder. If he could find out why Caroline Luard had been killed, he might also find the culprit. But after several days of talking to people who had known her, he had come up with nothing. If Caroline had had any secrets in her life, none of her friends or servants knew them.

She got on well with her husband, and he with her. She enjoyed her life, enjoyed her home, and her only tragedy was the untimely death of her younger son.

Without a motive, Taylor turned instead to the details of the murder. He was interested in the time it had taken Caroline Luard to walk from the wicket gate to the summer house. At a very slow stroll, the journey took forty-five minutes. At the sort of pace a woman of fifty-eight might have set, it took just short of thirty.

'And why is that important?' Warde asked him.

'It means there are fifteen minutes of this woman's life that we can't account for,' Taylor said. 'If she reached La Casa at three o'clock – but wasn't killed until 3.15 – what happened in the meantime?'

'Go on.'

'There are several options. She met someone there by chance, had a brief chat with him, and was clubbed and shot when she turned to leave.'

'But you don't like that?'

Taylor shook his head. 'Her body was facing the wrong way. For the same reason, I don't like the idea that she met someone there by prior agreement either. If the missing minutes were taken up in chat, why was she lying face down with her head pointing towards the summer house door?'

'Perhaps her killer left first.'

'She'd have turned to watch him go and

you'd have found her on her back with a punch to the face and a bullet between the eyes.'

'So what are the other options?' Warde asked.

Taylor ticked them off on his fingers. 'One – she met someone on the path, decided he was harmless, and offered to show him the summer house. He stood back to let her climb the steps ahead of him and knocked her out before she reached the door. Two – she was followed from the road but didn't realise it. For reasons of her own, she decided to inspect the summer house and was rushed from behind as soon as she stepped onto the veranda.'

'And with either of those, she would have lain unconscious during the missing minutes?'

Taylor nodded.

'It wouldn't have taken quarter of an hour to remove her glove and steal her rings.'

'No,' Taylor agreed. 'But an argument about what to do with her might.'

'Explain.'

'I think there was more than one person involved in this crime.'

*   *   *

. . . In conclusion, I believe events took place as follows:

Two or more villains were casing La Casa with a view to breaking into it. Had Mrs Luard arrived thirty minutes later, she would have found the door forced open and the interior ransacked. The aim may have been simple vandalism – to destroy something prized and owned by 'rich people'.

It was Mrs Luard's misfortune to reach the clearing in front of the summer house whilst one of the culprits was on the veranda. He may have tried to dodge out of sight around the corner of the building but I believe she saw him well enough to recognise him.

She had no reason to fear him otherwise she wouldn't have mounted the steps. This makes me think he was local. He may also have been young. A stranger, or an adult man, would have made her think twice about confronting him.

If the culprit was a local youth then Kent

police will have had dealings with him. He may have a father dead or in prison, and a mother who struggles to keep her children fed. It is often the case that a son, lacking the stern guidance of a father, rejects the control of his mother and turns to crime.

Such a family would have been known to Mrs Luard through her charity work. Her friends describe her as a confident and clever person with a genuine concern for the plight of widows and deserted wives. She went to their houses and watched their children grow up.

If she knew the trespasser, there's a good chance she took him to task. What was he up to? Why wasn't he at work? Did he think his mother wanted him to spend his days in idleness and crime?

Even if she guessed that he had a friend or friends in tow, she wasn't expecting one of them to come up behind her. She saw the trespasser as a layabout and a petty thief, not as a killer. Her mistake may have been to say that she was going to report him to the police.

The threat would have been taken seriously

by anyone who knew that Mrs Luard was the wife of a Justice of the Peace and a friend to the Chief Constable of Kent. To a stranger, she was just a woman walking through Frankfield Park. To a local good-for-nothing, she was a woman of status and influence.

I see this as a crime of stupidity and panic rather than a pre-set plan to murder Mrs Luard. Whether through hot-headedness or a desire to shut her up, the person behind her used the revolver as a club. It may be that both culprits were intoxicated and acted under the madness of alcohol.

Once the blow was struck, it could not be taken back. Simple trespass had become violent assault and Mrs Luard would be able to name at least one of her attackers. It is my belief that most of the missing fifteen minutes were taken up in an argument about what to do next. Leave her alive or kill her?

From the outset of this inquiry, police have been confused by the way Mrs Luard died. Was she murdered by a stranger or by someone she knew? Was her death the result of a bungled robbery? Or were her rings stolen to make it seem that way? Why was she shot twice when one bullet would have done?

I believe the answers to these questions are simple. She was killed by people she knew. They took her rings and purse to make it look as if the motive was robbery. If they were local, they would have known she wore rings on her left hand – which was the only glove that was removed.

The murder was planned in so far as a choice was made to kill her rather than leave her alive. Neither culprit was safe if she was able to name one of them. And neither culprit was prepared to go to prison for assaulting the wife of Major-General Luard.

To protect themselves, they took it in turns to fire into her brain. As long as they both played a part in her murder, they could rely on each other to keep quiet about what they had done.

If the killer or killers are local, there is a good chance the weapon is still in their possession. There is a good chance too that it was acquired during an earlier house burglary in the Ightham area.

I propose that Kent Police go back through their records of the last five years. If they find a description of a stolen .32 revolver, they will have reason to go house-to-house looking for it . . .

*   *   *

Henry Warde folded his hands over Taylor's report, which lay on the desk between them. 'I'll be lynched if I give an order to search every house,' he said. 'The people of Ightham will say I'd rather cast suspicion on them than admit my friend shot his wife.'

'It's a better line of inquiry than anything else we have.'

'Assuming you're right,' said Warde. 'But you're opening a can of worms with what you've written. You're asking me to come down hard on the poor for a crime that everyone thinks a rich man committed.'

'It's the only avenue we haven't explored,' Taylor pointed out. 'We've ignored Mrs Luard's neighbours – rich *and* poor – to focus on passing vagrants and hired killers.'

'They'll accuse me of framing an innocent person to get Charles off.'

'Maybe so, but our job is to find Mrs Luard's killer . . . not to treat the locals with kid gloves because we're afraid of what they might say.'

'They want him to hang. That's all they talk about in Ightham.'

Taylor pulled a crooked smile. 'I know. I've heard them. I keep wondering why it might be in someone's interests to blacken the Major-General. Who was the first to accuse him?'

Warde opened a drawer and took out three envelopes. 'These arrived for Charles yesterday,' he said, pushing them across the desk. 'I was in the house when they came, otherwise he'd have burnt them. He tells me he's had dozens . . . many with local postmarks.'

I know what you are.

I know what you like to do to women.

Make them cry. Make them squeal.

Twisted old man. Dirty old man.

Rot in Hell.

**YOU THINK YOU'RE ABOVE
THE REST OF US.**

**YOU THINK YOU HAVE THE
RIGHT TO JUDGE US.**

THIS IS THE SENTENCE WE GIVE YOU.

**KILL YOURSELF BEFORE THE
HANGMAN GETS YOU.**

You want people to think tramps
and gypos shot your wife.

We know different.

It was you.

You may have friends in high places
but God will be your judge.

Chapter Eight

Friday, 4 September 1908 –
Ightham, morning

A shroud of misery hung over Ightham Knoll when Taylor rang the doorbell on Friday morning. The maid who let him in was in tears, and the sound of weeping was coming from the kitchen.

He was shown into the drawing-room, where the Major-General was standing in front of his wife's portrait, head bowed and fingers pressed to his eyes. It was several seconds before he spoke. 'I've given the staff notice,' he said. 'They're very upset about it.'

'It's a difficult time for all of you,' Taylor answered tactfully. He'd been told by Henry

Warde that Luard had made up his mind to leave Ightham and rent a house somewhere else.

'I've ordered everything to be sold – the house, the contents . . . *everything.*' The old man's voice shook with emotion as he lowered himself into a chair. 'It's all too painful. I can't bear to be reminded of her.'

Sergeant, the fox terrier, dropped to the floor at his master's feet, and Taylor wondered if the dog, too, was up for sale. He thought the Major-General's decision a bad one. It smacked too much of flight and a ruthless desire to kill every memory of Caroline.

'What about your son?' he asked, taking a seat himself. 'Will he feel the same?'

Luard looked towards a photograph of a young man in uniform. 'He's with the Army in South Africa. Soldiers travel light.'

'But I'm told he's on a steamer coming home . . . due to arrive in two weeks. Shouldn't you wait until he gets here?'

With a groan of despair, the Major-General dropped his head into his hands. 'What for? Do you think I want him to hear what's being said about me or read the poison that pours through my letter box every day? It would break his spirit the way it's broken mine.'

Taylor leaned forward. 'I wish you'd told us about the letters when they first started coming,' he said gently. 'We would have advised you not to open them.'

'Then I wouldn't have opened the kind ones either. Not everyone is cruel.'

Taylor allowed a short silence to develop while he worked out how to ask his next question. 'People often write the way they speak,' he said. 'Did any of the phrases in the cruel letters give you a sense of who might have written them?'

Luard shook his head. 'They all say the same thing. That I killed my wife to be with another woman.' He raised tired eyes to Taylor's. 'I'm nearly seventy years old and I enjoyed being with Caroline. Why would I have wanted anyone else?'

'A poison pen letter doesn't speak the truth, sir. The only aim of the writer is to hurt. When did the first one arrive?'

The old man thought for a moment. 'The evening of the first inquest.'

'Do you remember the postmark?'

'I believe it was Ightham. I recall being shocked that someone nearby could have written something so unkind.'

'Then the sender may have been in this room when the evidence was given,' Taylor told him. He recalled the crowd of locals who had thronged into the Luards' house that day. 'Do you think your maids would be able to put together a list of the people who were here?'

Luard gave a weary shake of his head. 'Why bother? It's of no interest to me. I shan't be here much longer. Henry Warde's brother has offered me a bed so the letters won't reach me.'

Somehow Taylor doubted that. The Chief Constable's brother was the local MP, and the gossips would find out all too fast that yet another member of the Kent ruling class was stepping in to help the Major-General. But, as Henry Warde had said, where else could the poor fellow go? The only family Charles had left was a son on a ship coming home from South Africa.

Taylor stayed for another thirty minutes,

keeping Luard company. He was shocked at how depressed the Major-General was, and he wondered why Henry Warde hadn't done something about the hate mail earlier.

In all his years at Scotland Yard, Taylor had never seen neighbours turn so cruelly on one of their own. It made him wonder yet again what lay beneath the surface in Ightham.

*　*　*

Before he left, he had a quiet word with the housemaid, Jane Pugmore. She nodded when he asked her to make a list of anyone she remembered from the inquest. 'It'll take me an hour or two,' she told him. 'You'll have to call back this afternoon.'

Taylor nodded.

'I heard what some of the women said when they were leaving,' she went on. 'That they only came to see the house.'

He eyed her curiously. 'None of them had been here before?'

Jane looked scornful. 'They weren't the type that Mrs Luard entertained. And if you ask

76

me, they shouldn't have been allowed at the inquest either.'

'It's a public event. Anyone has the right to attend.'

'Not if it's to revel in a lady's death, they don't. I wouldn't mind so much if they'd listened to what was said instead of making up so-called evidence afterwards. A man can't be in two places at the same time . . . though you wouldn't think it to hear the nonsense that's being talked in the village.'

'What sort of nonsense?'

'*Every* sort,' she said crossly. 'It makes me so mad. They whisper behind their hands when they see me coming. But not one of them has ever asked me what *I* think.'

'And what's that, Jane?'

She glanced towards the drawing-room door. 'The Major-General's lost without his wife. He'd have died in her place if he could.'

*   *   *

Taylor's next visit was to a friend of Caroline Luard's. He had spoken to most of the others –

with little success – but Mrs Anderson had been absent the first time he tried to see her. Taylor wouldn't have gone back if she hadn't written to Henry Warde, urging him to send a policeman to speak to her.

Like Mary Stewart, she lived in a house overlooking the village green. But that was as far as the likeness between the two women went. Sarah Anderson was sixty-five and had no time for women who threw fainting fits. She was short and stocky, didn't wear corsets, and spoke her mind in a forthright manner.

She pointed to a chair when Taylor was shown into her sitting-room. 'Sit down,' she said briskly, 'and tell me how I can help. If I understood Mary Stewart correctly, in between her fainting fits, you asked her for the names of ne'er-do-wells that Caroline met through her charity work.'

Taylor was amused by her bluntness. 'It's one line of inquiry,' he explained. 'We can't discount that her killer might have been a local man.'

'If you listen to the gossip on the streets of Ightham, the local man was Caroline's husband,

Charles. They say he shot her because he was having an affair with a woman in the village.'

'But you don't agree?'

'Hardly! Charles would never do anything so vulgar as to murder his wife. He's a typical Army officer . . . likes to conform and follow the rules.'

'What about having an affair?'

Mrs Anderson gave a small laugh. 'Same answer. He's too afraid of scandal to go running after bits of skirt in his own back garden.'

Taylor smiled at her choice of words. 'So where did the rumours come from?'

'It's a good question. I asked my parlourmaid if she'd ever heard them before Caroline died, and she said no. They seem to have grown out of this absurd belief that Charles was the killer. Without a reason for why he might want to shoot his wife, people have invented one.'

Taylor watched her for a moment. 'It's quite a witch hunt that's been whipped up against him. Have you any idea who started it?'

She shook her head. 'You'll have to go to the pubs for that. My servants tell me they talk about nothing else in the George & Dragon.'

'And they all think the Major-General's guilty?'

'As far as I can tell.' She paused. 'It's his own fault. He turned up his nose at the common people and left Caroline to deal with them. Now they've turned *her* into a saint and *him* into the devil.'

'Was she a saint?'

'Of course not. She was as snobbish as he is.'

'But knew better how to hide it?'

'Indeed.' Sarah Anderson stood up and went to a desk in the corner of the room. 'I've made a list of families who fall into the sort of group I think you're looking for. They come from a wide area. In most cases, the wives have been abandoned to bring up their children alone . . . but the last two have husbands who become violent when they drink.'

Taylor read the names and addresses. One of the families came from Ightham but the rest were in nearby villages like Stone Street or Borough Green. 'Have you noticed any of these people acting oddly since the murder, Mrs Anderson?'

'In what way?'

'Out of character . . . different from normal.'

She shook her head. 'They're always on their best behaviour with me. It's the only way they can be sure of getting money.'

Taylor folded the paper and tucked it into his pocket. 'They should be grateful you're keeping them out of the workhouse.'

Mrs Anderson gave a dry smile. 'Do you think so, Superintendent? For myself, I don't enjoy watching hard-pressed women bow and scrape just to put food in their children's mouths. We should have found a way by now to give the poor a little dignity instead of asking them to beg.'

Chapter Nine

Friday, 4 September 1908 –
George & Dragon, midday

No one turned to look at Taylor as he walked into the dimly lit saloon bar of the George & Dragon. But he didn't doubt the other customers were aware of his presence and knew who he was. Within minutes, most of what they said was being aimed at him.

There were too many comments about the police turning a blind eye to 'a certain person' and the murder inquiry being a 'farce'. Several times, the Chief Constable was referred to as a rich man's 'stooge' and the police as 'useless'.

Taylor folded his felt hat and tucked it into

his pocket, giving a friendly nod to the land-lord. He ordered a pint and leant on the bar while the man pulled his beer. 'Did any of your customers attend the first inquest?' he asked.

'What if they did?'

Taylor shrugged amiably. 'They'd know the Major-General has an alibi for the time of his wife's death.'

The landlord glared at him, clearly on the side of his customers. 'No one believes it.'

Taylor took a sip of beer. 'So who's the loud-mouth in the corner? He seems to have a down on anyone connected to the case.'

The landlord flicked a cloth across the bar. 'John Farrell. He's only saying what he believes. Nothing wrong with that.'

'Until he incites a lynch mob to hang the Major-General from the nearest tree,' Taylor replied, flicking a glance at the big man who was holding court at the far table. Whenever he spoke, the lesser men around him listened. 'What's his problem with Luard? Why is he so hostile?'

'Same as the rest of us . . . reckons the old brute is getting away with murder.'

'Except brutality doesn't come out of nowhere. Did the Major-General make a habit of assaulting his wife? Does he beat his servants when they annoy him?'

A hush fell over the room as if the other drinkers had decided to listen. The landlord shrugged. 'Not that I'm aware of.'

'No,' Taylor agreed. 'They seem quite fond of him. It makes you wonder what his wife could have done that made him angry enough to shoot her.'

'He was bored with her.'

Taylor used his finger to wipe a trickle of froth from the side of his glass. 'But why blow her brains out so close to home?' he asked mildly. 'If he'd waited a few days until they were on holiday, he could have pushed her off a cliff. Everyone would have believed it was an accident.'

There was a brief silence before John Farrell's voice broke in from the corner. 'He wouldn't have had the Chief Constable's help in any other county.'

With a lazy smile, Taylor turned towards him. 'If that were true, I wouldn't be here, Mr

Farrell,' he said. 'You can't have it both ways. If Henry Warde was trying to protect his friend, he wouldn't have called in Scotland Yard.'

The man spat on the floor. 'You don't know your arse from your elbow, mate. If you did, you'd have arrested the old bugger by now.'

His words were greeted with a snigger by the other men at his table.

Taylor eyed him for a moment then took out his tobacco pouch and calmly rolled a cigarette. 'It's quite a campaign you've got going against the Major-General,' he murmured, running the edge of the paper across his tongue. 'Did you start it or are you just mouthing someone else's ideas?'

'None of your business. It's a free country. I can say what I like when I like.'

Taylor lit a match and held it to the tip of his cigarette. 'Even when you're wrong? What if I say *you* killed Mrs Luard and you're putting the blame on the Major-General to avoid being hanged yourself?'

'You'd get my fist in your face.'

Taylor shook out the match and flipped it onto the counter. 'You have a bad temper, my friend. Do you lash out at everyone who annoys you?'

'I don't take lip if that's what you mean. No man does.' Farrell dropped a wink at one of his friends. 'Except for the nancy boys at Scotland Yard who think they're the cat's bloody whiskers in their smart coats and pretty hats.'

Taylor blew a smoke ring into the air. 'You're a big man. I doubt you're challenged very often.'

'That's the truth of it. Do you fancy your chances?'

Taylor shook his head. 'I see too much violence in my job . . . and it's usually aimed at women. The only way a stupid man can control his wife is by using her as a punchbag. We see a lot of that in the poorer parts of London.'

Farrell's face turned a dark red. 'What are you implying?'

'That the most likely type to have killed Mrs Luard is a drunken brute who makes a habit of beating women. He enjoys the power it gives him to see the fear in their eyes.' Taylor smiled slightly. 'Would you say that's a good description of Major-General Luard?'

The question was greeted with silence.

Taylor pulled his hat from his pocket and pushed out the crown before placing it on his head. 'Give my regards to your wife and ask her to expect me later today. Shall we say five o'clock? I need to talk to you in private, Mr Farrell.'

The man looked uneasy. 'Why?'

'You seem to know so much about Mrs Luard's murder.' He tipped the brim of his hat to the other men at the table. 'I'll be calling on you all in the next few days, gentlemen. We can't hold a second inquest until we have all the facts.'

As he left, he was amused by the sounds of dismay that broke out behind him. He trod out his cigarette and double-checked the last name on Sarah Anderson's list. *'John Farrell,'* she'd written in neat handwriting. *'He punches his wife and children when he's drunk.'*

* * *

Taylor tapped on the tradesmen's entrance to Ightham Knoll because he didn't want to disturb Charles Luard again. Jane Pugmore, the housemaid, let him in and took him to the kitchen, where Cook and Harriet Huish, the parlourmaid, were still red-eyed from weeping.

Cook showed him the Major-General's uneaten lunch. 'He's hardly touched his food since Mrs Luard died,' she said. 'He's that low, he's making himself ill.' She picked up the plate and made to scrape the contents into a slop bucket.

Taylor put his hand on her arm. 'Don't waste it,' he begged. 'I haven't had a decent meal since I arrived in Kent.'

The three women threw up their arms in horror and bustled around to take his coat and lay a place for him at the table. Jane pressed the Superintendent into a chair and gave him the list she'd made of people who had attended the first inquest. It was much longer than Sarah Anderson's and, while he ate, Taylor asked the three women to mark which of the names would be most likely to write poison pen letters.

He was surprised at how easy they found it to agree. They picked only women, and the comments they made while they did it told him why. 'Bitter old spinster' . . . 'guzzles sherry in secret' . . . 'jealous as sin' . . . 'man-hater' . . .

One or two were ladies who claimed to have been friends of Caroline Luard, but most were what Jane Pugmore described scornfully as the lower middle class. 'They think they're above us servants,' she told Taylor, 'but it eats away at them that they're not in the Major-General's league.'

He ran his finger down the page. 'I wonder why poison pen letters are usually written by women,' he murmured.

'Because they marry husbands they don't like and spend the rest of their lives picking fault with them,' said Cook bluntly. 'It turns them nasty.'

'So why marry them in the first place?'

'To give themselves airs and graces. The man who owns the shop that sells the cabbages is higher up the ladder than the one who grows them . . . which is what their fathers did.' Cook poured water into the sink. 'Most of the cats on that list are no better than I am, but you wouldn't think it from the way they look down their noses at me.'

It was the second time in three hours that Taylor had heard a woman express discontent about the way her society worked. Yet he wondered if either of them would have voiced her thoughts out loud before Caroline Luard's murder.

Had Caroline's friend, Sarah Anderson, always wanted dignity for the poor? Or was it the shock of her friend's death that had set her thinking about the divide between the classes? Had Cook always resented women who married above themselves? Or was she simply trying to account for the hate mail that kept dropping through the letter box?

It seemed to Superintendent Taylor that Ightham's sleepy calm had been ripped apart by a couple of gunshots. As if a close-knit family had turned on itself because no one believed the victim had been killed by an outsider. Instead of peace, there was war. Instead of mutual support, there was suspicion.

'Could it have been someone from round here who killed Mrs Luard?' he asked.

There was a brief silence before Harriet Huish spoke.

'Put it this way,' she said, 'there's plenty more likely to have done it than the Major-General.'

'Someone like John Farrell, perhaps?'

Cook made a scornful noise in her throat. 'It's a miracle his wife's still alive,' she said. 'He's a nasty piece of work, and his son's just as bad.'

'How old is he?'

'Will Farrell? Seventeen . . . eighteen. He goes out poaching with Michael Blaine from Stone Street. They're as vicious as snakes and as idle as the day is long.'

Chapter Ten

Friday, 4 September 1908 –
Ightham, afternoon

Taylor made his way to Miss Amy Pegg's house in the High Street. She was the 'bitter old spinster' of Jane Pugmore's list, and Taylor understood why when he realised how lonely the woman was.

She invited him into her parlour and he wished he had his constable with him. There was something slightly mad about the way the woman behaved. One minute she was cowering away, the next she was flashing her eyes at him like an ageing flirt.

He wondered if her mind had gone, because she seemed to think he wanted to hear her life story. She told him rambling tales about growing up in Ightham, claiming Charles Luard had been her 'childhood sweetheart' before Caroline had stolen him away.

She seemed unaware that the Luards had been married for thirteen years before they moved to Ightham Knoll, and that neither of them had lived in Kent before.

But it wasn't until she claimed she was giving 'dear Charles' all the help she could 'at this difficult time' that Taylor held up his hand. 'We both know that's not true, Miss Pegg. The only people helping him are his close friends and servants.'

Her face became spiteful. 'You mean Henry Warde, I suppose. He'd say black was white to protect Charles.'

'That's not true either,' said Taylor. 'You might as well accuse the police from Scotland Yard of not doing their job properly. Are you accusing *me*, Miss Pegg?'

She wrapped her arms across her thin chest. 'I don't know who you are,' she whined. 'You're a bully. I'm afraid of you.'

Taylor took the hate letters from his pocket. 'The only bullies round here are people who write poison like this. Do you want to explain why you're one of them?'

She stared at him with mad-looking eyes. 'I'm doing God's work.'

* * *

Taylor was left with a nasty taste in his mouth. All he'd done was pry into the misery of an unhappy woman. He had no better luck with the next person on Jane's list – the secret sherry guzzler.

She was fat and florid, slurred her words and told him she knew for a fact that Caroline Luard had gone to the summer house to meet a younger lover. The Major-General followed in secret and shot his wife out of jealousy when he caught her 'at it'.

Taylor didn't believe this sexual fantasy any more than he believed that Miss Pegg had been Charles's childhood sweetheart. There would have been two bodies on the veranda floor if Luard had fired his gun in the heat of anger. It was a rare husband who killed his wife but spared his rival.

As Superintendent Taylor emerged into the fresh air, he made a mental note to listen the next time his wife told him she was bored and wanted a job. It clearly wasn't healthy to sit alone with nothing to do all day.

The irony of that thought hit him when he reached John Farrell's door at five o'clock. The woman who opened it looked very ill, but not from under-work, he thought. She had a yellow bruise around one of her eyes, and was surrounded by half-starved, pale-faced children.

Taylor didn't need the smell of wet washing in the tiny house, or the sheets hanging on the line outside, to tell him she took in laundry for a living. The only time her hands were out of water, he guessed, was when she was asleep.

He explained who he was and asked if her husband was at home. Mrs Farrell nodded to a curtained alcove in the corner of the room. 'It's best not to wake him.'

'He knows I'm coming.'

'Don't make no difference. He has a bad temper when he's in drink.'

'We'll see,' said Taylor, stepping inside the door.

There was only one room on the ground floor, though some rickety steps in the corner suggested a bedroom upstairs. Taylor pulled the curtain aside to expose John Farrell, fully clothed and flat on his back on a stained mattress. He nudged the man with his foot but got no response.

'You have my sympathy, Mrs Farrell,' he said loudly. 'You made a rotten bargain when you picked this one.'

If he hadn't been ready for it, the man's speed would have taken him by surprise. Farrell launched himself off the mattress in a roaring charge, fists flying.

'A *very* bad bargain,' Taylor grunted, jabbing his knee into Farrell's groin and crowding him back against the wall. He slammed his forearm against the man's throat. 'A brute when he's drunk and a fool when he's sober.'

The woman wrung her hands. 'He'll take it out on me and the kids if you don't let him go,' she wailed.

'He'll do that anyway,' said Taylor, staring into the other man's eyes. 'He doesn't need reasons to inflict pain.'

'You don't know him like I do, sir. He can be nice when he wants.'

The Superintendent wondered why battered women always said the same. It made no sense to him. He eased the pressure on the other man's throat. 'Does your husband own a revolver, Mrs Farrell?'

He heard the sudden tremor in her voice. 'He wasn't the one shot Mrs Luard, sir. He was here with me when the poor lady died.'

'And you'll swear to that on the Bible, I suppose?'

'It's the truth.'

'I doubt it. The truth is he'll beat you within an inch of your life if you don't lie for him.' Taylor dropped his arm and stepped away. 'You're a better fit for a woman-killer than the Major-General, Mr Farrell.'

'You heard the wife,' the man growled. 'It wasn't me. What business would I have had in Frankfield Park that day?'

'A better question would be, what business did you have here at 3.15 on a Monday afternoon? Why weren't you out working?'

'Times are hard.'

'Is that right? So where did your beer money come from in the pub this lunchtime? Did you pawn a couple of stolen rings, perhaps?'

Farrell wasn't used to fighting men. He signalled his moves in advance and looked surprised when Taylor dodged. The Superintendent easily landed a punch in the pit of the lumbering oaf's stomach, but it was hardly a fair contest. Farrell was drunk, and Taylor had been a champion boxer in his day.

The man doubled up, winded. 'Why are you doing this?' he whined. 'It wasn't me killed Mrs Luard.' He flicked an assessing glance at his wife. 'It's the ones who were out and about you should be after.'

Taylor felt – rather than saw – the woman's sudden movement. He glanced round and watched her grab the wrist of the thin-faced youth who was standing beside her. The boy looked scared, and it seemed to Taylor that his mother was trying to keep him from running.

'It's you who keeps picking the fight,' Taylor told Farrell. 'I'm just defending myself.'

The man made a retching sound. 'Yeah, well, you'd better be watching your back from now on.'

'You interest me more and more, Mr Farrell. Is that how you usually attack a person? From behind?'

There was a short silence before the woman spoke. 'You have to believe me, sir. John was sleeping off the drink . . . like he does every afternoon.'

Taylor eyed her for a moment then shifted his gaze to the youth. 'Is this Will? What about him? Where was he when Mrs Luard was shot?'

The woman tightened her grip on the lad's wrist. 'He was here,' she said in a shaky voice. 'I can't do the laundry without him.'

* * *

Taylor's last visit that day was to Ightham police station. He expected the local bobby to be manning the desk, but instead he found George Hamble sorting through some notes.

Taylor propped his shoulder against the wall. 'Anything new?' he asked.

The Inspector shook his head. 'What about your end?'

'I don't know yet.' Taylor took Sarah Anderson's list from his pocket and placed it on the desk. 'Have you come across any of these families?'

The other man glanced at the names. 'Every copper in the district knows them.'

'For what?'

'Drunk and disorderly . . . petty theft . . . trespass . . . vandalism. They take up more police time than everyone else round here put together. Why are you interested?'

'Whoever shot Mrs Luard probably has a history of criminal behaviour. It's a big step from honest citizen to ruthless murderer.'

The Inspector gave a dry laugh. 'Unless she was killed by a jealous husband who also happens to be a Justice of the Peace.'

Taylor shook his head. 'There'd still be a history. The Major-General would have given her a black eye every time she tried to lock him out of her bedroom.'

Hamble placed his hand on the list. 'There are some bad apples here but I can't see any of them shooting Mrs Luard. They wouldn't have dared. Country folk have more respect for their betters than city dwellers.'

Taylor moved to the window. Dusk was falling quickly but he could see a little knot of serving girls, hurrying to buy bread before the baker closed for the night. Here and there, flickering candles shone through ground-floor windows. In the gathering darkness he might have been looking at a street in the East End.

'What if a woman like Mrs Luard was murdered in Hyde Park, George? Where do you think we'd be looking for her murderer? Out here in the wilds of Kent or somewhere in London?'

'London.'

'Even closer. We'd be looking for people who lived and worked in the Hyde Park area. Criminals tend to operate close to home because they know the best escape routes.'

'Our man had two and a half hours to disappear.'

'Maybe so, but don't you find it odd that a

stranger managed to enter and leave Frankfield Park without being seen? How did he get there? On foot? On a bicycle? Which direction did he come from? Several people saw the Major-General but no one remembers a stranger.'

'No one remembers the people on this list either.'

'How do you know?' Taylor turned from the window. 'Has anyone even been asked that question?'

Chapter Eleven

Saturday, 5 September 1908 –
Stone Street, morning

Saturday morning broke cold and clear, and the Scotland Yard detectives put on extra vests to travel by pony and trap. They planned to start in the village of Stone Street before moving on to Borough Green and the other places beyond Ightham.

Kent's police chief, Henry Warde, had refused the London visitors the use of his Daimler because it was too well known. Asking questions of the poor and needy was Superintendent Taylor's line of inquiry. If Scotland Yard came up with anything, Kent Police would take the credit. If they didn't, Warde would deny that the poor had ever been his target.

Stone Street was a smaller village than Ightham, clustered on the southern border of Frankfield Park. For that reason the people who lived there were of interest to Taylor. In particular, one family on Sarah Anderson's list.

'*Mrs Blaine,*' she had written. '*Three young children, husband in prison, and an older stepson, Michael (20). She's afraid of him.*'

'What's the plan?' Constable Philpott asked as the village came into view.

Taylor ordered the driver to stop and jumped down from the seat. The broadleaf woodland of Frankfield Park ran along the other side of the road, and some five hundred yards ahead on the right, he could just make out the turning that led to St Lawrence's Church and the wicket gate where the Luards had separated for the last time.

'We'll go to house-to-house,' he told Philpott. 'I want the name or description of anyone seen walking along this road on the 24th August, including the people who live here.'

Memories were surprisingly good. As several

villagers said, it focused the mind to have a murder on the doorstep. The same names cropped up again and again. Various tradesmen. The baker's boy on his bicycle. The butcher's cart delivering meat. The farrier coming to shoe one of Mr Wallace's horses. The vicar in his car.

One or two claimed to have seen Major-General Luard and Sergeant emerge from Church Road and turn towards Godden Green. But of more interest to Taylor, an elderly farm worker said he had noticed Michael Blaine heading up the same road some two hours earlier.

'Did you see him come back?' the Superintendent asked.

'Never do. Stays out till all hours.'

'Where does he work?'

The old man shrugged. 'You'll have to ask him. I don't pry into other people's affairs.'

'Does he go out poaching?'

'Not my place to say.'

Taylor put a hand on the door to keep it open. 'Are you afraid of Michael Blaine?'

There was a tiny pause. 'His stepmother is.'

With a sudden push he shut the policeman out of the house.

The Blaines' house – a wooden shack – stood at the end of a rutted lane, on the other side of the road from the Church Road turning. It was a quarter the size of the summer house at Frankfield House, had no windows and was in a bad state of repair. The rickety front door stood open to let some light in.

'I'd probably want to vandalise La Casa myself if I lived in a dump like this,' Philpott muttered to his boss as the pair of detectives approached.

Taylor was thinking the same. He rapped his knuckles on the door frame. 'Mrs Blaine,' he called, peering into the gloomy interior. 'I'm Superintendent Taylor of Scotland Yard and this is Constable Philpott. May we come in?'

There was a scurry of movement before a woman appeared in front of them. Her alarm was obvious but she did her best to hide it. She tried to keep the two men outside but Taylor had already stepped over the threshold.

'We're asking everyone in Stone Street where they were and who they saw on the day Mrs

Luard died,' he told her. He smiled at the three little urchins who clustered around her skirt. 'Were you out playing that day, kids? Do you remember seeing the Major-General and his dog?'

'They don't know nothing,' said Mrs Blaine, shooing the children outside. 'None of us does.'

She threw a worried look towards the corner of the room and Taylor followed her gaze. He made out the figure of a young man, standing in the shadows. His hair looked tousled as if he'd just got up. 'You must be Michael,' said Taylor.

'What if I am?'

The Superintendent produced one of his lazy smiles. 'I'm told you do labouring jobs at Frankfield Park from time to time.'

'Maybe.'

'Were you there when Mrs Luard was killed?'

'No. Last time they needed me was July. You can check it in their records.'

Taylor nodded. 'So who was employing you on the 24th?' His eyes were adjusting to the dimness and he could see the rigid set of the youngster's shoulders and jawline.

'Can't remember . . . could have been any-one.'

'Give me some names,' Taylor said, taking his notebook and pencil from his pocket.

'He was here with me,' Mrs Blaine blurted out. 'Ain't that right, Michael?'

'Yeah.'

Taylor shook his head. 'You were seen walking up Church Road at about 12.30. Where were you going?'

A look of hostility glittered in Blaine's eyes. He wasn't used to having his movements questioned by anyone. 'I sure as hell wasn't going to Frankfield Park.'

Taylor flipped to the front of his notebook. 'You were at the summer house the next morning. One of the constables took your name.'

'So? It wasn't just me that was curious.'

'How come you weren't working that day either?' Taylor glanced around the cramped room. There was a mattress for the mother and younger children, a couple of wooden chairs and a folded blanket which was probably what Blaine rolled himself up in at night. 'It looks

108

to me as if your stepmother needs every penny you can earn.'

'We get by.'

'Only through the kindness of ladies like Mrs Luard.' Taylor turned back to the woman. 'You must be worried her charities won't help you now that she's dead.'

Mrs Blaine looked away, unable to meet his eye. 'Her husband should hang for what he did.'

'Except it wasn't the Major-General who murdered her, Mrs Blaine. She was attacked by two men, and one of them had a revolver. We think the weapon was stolen from a house in this area.'

There was no response.

'The man with the revolver used the butt to club Mrs Luard down. She lay unconscious for several minutes before he and his friend decided to shoot her.' He turned to Michael Blaine. 'It was a stupid and vicious crime,' he said. 'The sort that low-grade vermin commit.'

The young man took a step forward, balling his fists. 'Save your breath. What happened over there was nothing to do with me.'

Taylor ignored him. 'The only reason Mrs Luard is dead is because she knew her killers. We're looking for local men – aged between seventeen and twenty – with a history of thieving and poaching. There's no trust between them. They took it in turns to fire into her head so that if one of them hangs they both will.'

He watched the colour drain from Mrs Blaine's face and saw the speed with which her stepson gripped her arm in an iron fist in case she tried to speak. 'I guess it's true what everyone's saying,' Michael hissed. 'You'll make a poor man swing rather than the bastard she married. You've already been after Will Farrell. Now you think you can come after me.'

Taylor stared him down. 'The Major-General can prove he was halfway to Godden Green when his wife was shot. Can you do the same?'

'I don't have to. It wasn't me that killed her.'

'Then you'd better hope Will Farrell stays quiet. I gave him an easy ride yesterday.'

'You've got nothing on either of us.'

Taylor glanced around the room. 'So it won't matter to you if we search this place?'

'Like hell you will,' Blaine snarled. 'Where's your warrant? We've got the same rights as the rich.'

'What are you afraid we're going to find, Michael?'

'Nothing. I'm afraid of what you'll plant on me. You think you can treat us like dirt just because we're poor. Mrs Luard was the same. She made us beg for every penny she handed out.'

'You've never begged in your life,' Taylor said coldly. 'You send your stepmother out to do it for you. The world is full of worthless layabouts who'd rather be kept by women than lift a finger for themselves.'

The youth's eyes narrowed angrily. 'You don't know nothing.'

Taylor turned towards the door. 'I know this. Mrs Luard would still be alive if she'd left you to starve in the workhouse.'

Chapter Twelve

Saturday, 5 September 1908 –
Sevenoaks, late evening

Henry Warde threaded his way through the saloon bar of the Farmer's Inn to where Taylor and Philpott were sitting. The Superintendent slid a pint of ale across the table. 'Drink up,' he said. 'We're two ahead of you.'

Kent's Chief Constable put his hat on the table and sat down. 'How did it go?'

'So-so. We're frozen to death but we visited every family on Mrs Anderson's list. Most of them allowed us to search their houses. The further we drove from Ightham the more willing they were to let us look.'

'Did you find anything?'

Taylor shook his head.

'So it was a waste of time?'

'Not exactly.' Taylor took out his notebook. 'It's all in here. The most likely culprits are Michael Blaine and Will Farrell. We'll need warrants to search their houses but I doubt we'll find anything.'

Warde took a mouthful of beer and ran his eye over Taylor's notes. 'There's a sighting of Blaine near Frankfield Park . . . two or three witnesses claiming that Blaine and Farrell go poaching together . . . and someone who says he knows Farrell wasn't at home on the 24th.' He shook his head. 'We can't arrest them on this.'

'Not for murder,' Taylor agreed, 'but Will Farrell's scared out of his wits. I might be able to crack him if we can bring him in on a poaching charge.'

'How?'

'By persuading him that whoever fired the second shot isn't guilty of murder. You can't kill someone who's already dead.'

Warde frowned. 'That's no defence in law. If there were two of them, they were jointly to blame for what happened.'

'But Will might avoid the noose if he gives us Blaine. A good barrister will argue that he only fired because he was afraid Blaine would kill him if he refused.'

'How do you know it was Blaine who shot first?'

'I don't, but I can't see him taking orders from a seventeen-year-old. Michael Blaine's a much stronger character than Will Farrell. If Michael hadn't wanted Mrs Luard dead, the murder wouldn't have happened.'

Warde toyed with the pages of the notebook. 'It's a good theory,' he said, 'but that's all it is. What if you're wrong?'

Taylor opened his tobacco pouch. 'The case will never be solved,' he said, smoothing a cigarette paper on the table. 'We're out of leads and out of ideas.'

* * *

It wasn't in Henry Warde's nature to make a decision in a hurry. As the next day was Sunday – and all good people would be in church – he said he'd use the rest of the weekend to think about it.

He was worried about the political fallout if Taylor's plan backfired. The newspapers would have a field day if the Kent Police arrested a youth on a trumped-up charge for the sole purpose of getting him to confess to a crime he didn't commit.

Perhaps Taylor should have insisted, but he'd learnt by now that it was better to let Warde reach a decision for himself. And, in truth, he was as keen to have a day off as the Chief Constable. He caught the last train to London to spend twenty-four hours with his wife and children, and quelled any doubts that his suspects would vanish.

The news that both Blaine and Farrell had been absent from their homes since Saturday night greeted him when he arrived at Warde's office on Monday morning. The Chief Constable was surprisingly cheerful about it. He took their flight as proof of guilt and told Taylor it was only a matter of time before they were caught.

Taylor had no such certainty. He helped draw up descriptions for the neighbouring police forces, but it was a fine example of closing the stable door after the horse had bolted. With a start of thirty-six hours, the youths had had plenty of time to disappear.

It was Taylor's view that they'd have gone to ground in London. And he knew there was little chance of finding them in the cramped and crowded tenements of Whitechapel or Blackfriars.

With no evidence to support Taylor's theory – and in face of Mrs Blaine's and Mrs Farrell's continued insistence that both youths had been at home on the day of the murder – Kent Police posted them as 'wanted for poaching' and kept their real reason for being interested in the pair to themselves.

The second inquest into Mrs Luard's death was held a few days later in the George & Dragon. It ended as the first had done, without a verdict. But this time it was Henry Warde who was to blame. Convinced that Blaine and Farrell would be found, he told the Coroner that Kent Police expected to make an arrest before the week was out and asked for another delay.

It was a mistake.

When no arrest happened, the gossips busied

themselves on why the Chief Constable of Kent had wanted to silence the Coroner yet again. Suspicion deepened when it became public knowledge that Major-General Luard was leaving Ightham for good on 16 September.

Was he fleeing Kent to avoid a murder charge? Had the Chief Constable realised that he couldn't protect his friend for ever?

*   *   *

Taylor looked up in surprise when Henry Warde was shown into his office on the afternoon of 17 September. He had spoken to the man by telephone only the day before and Warde had made no mention of a trip to the city.

He stood up to shake the Chief Constable's hand. 'There's nothing to add to what I told you yesterday,' Taylor said with regret. 'London's a big place. If Blaine and Farrell are here, no one's seen them.'

Warde lowered himself into a chair. He looked tired and depressed. 'That's not why I came.' He took a folded piece of paper from his breast pocket and handed it to the Superintendent.

'Charles Luard killed himself this morning. He left me this letter.'

Taylor stared at him in shock. *'Killed* himself?' he echoed. 'How? Why? I thought he was staying with your brother.'

'He was. He wrote some letters during the night then left early this morning to throw himself under a train.' He gestured towards the folded paper. 'He explains it in there.'

My dear Henry,

I am sorry to return your kindness and long friendship in this way, but I feel it is best to join Caroline in the second life at once. I am tired and I do not want to live any longer.

I thought I was strong enough to bear up against the terrible letters that arrive every day. But I find I am not. The dreadful murder of my wife has robbed me of all my happiness.

The sympathy of so many friends kept me going for a while but in this last day something seems to have snapped. The strength has left me and I care for nothing except to be with her again.

So goodbye, dear friend,

Charles

Taylor rested his forehead in his hands. 'We let him down. We should have realised he was as much a victim of the murder as his wife was.'

'He told my brother he'd lost hope of anyone being convicted.'

With a sigh, Taylor opened his bottom drawer and took out a bottle of brandy and a couple of glasses. 'What about the Luards' son?' He filled the glasses and pushed one across the desk. 'Didn't you tell me his ship was due to dock in Southampton this afternoon?'

Warde nodded. 'Poor fellow. He's barely had time to come to terms with his mother's death, and now he has to learn of his father's.' He reached for his glass and downed the contents in a single gulp. 'If Charles had waited, the lad might have persuaded him out of it.'

Taylor lifted his own glass and warmed the liquid between his hands. 'It's kinder this way. If your friend had killed himself anyway, his son would have had to bear the guilt.'

'Perhaps.'

'Was one of the letters addressed to him?'

Warde nodded. 'The others are to Caroline's family in Cumberland and the staff at their home at Ightham Knoll. There was also one for my brother.' Warde nodded to the page in front of Taylor. 'It said similar things to mine.'

A picture of the Major-General, writing letters by gaslight, sprang into Taylor's mind. It was a sad and lonely image. An old man quietly doing a last duty by his son and friends before he killed himself.

'You have to make this public,' Scotland Yard's Taylor urged, pushing the page across the desk. 'If you don't, his enemies will claim he killed himself out of guilt. Or worse, that he left a confession which you and your brother have suppressed.'

Warde reached for the brandy bottle. 'They'll claim it anyway,' he said bitterly. 'Publishing what he wrote won't convince them he was innocent. The only way to do that is to prove someone else was guilty.'

But, as both men now feared, that would never happen.

Epilogue

The final inquest into Caroline Luard's death ruled that she'd been murdered by 'person or persons unknown'. The verdict on her husband's death was that he had committed suicide while 'temporarily insane'.

The Coroner said that the Major-General had been driven to kill himself by the hate mail he received. Those who believed him innocent were shocked at how much cruelty had been shown by his neighbours. Those who believed him guilty thought he'd received his just deserts.

The letters he wrote in the hours before his death were read out at his inquest and published later in the local newspapers. Some found them moving and sincere, others thought they were a final, dishonest attempt by Major-General Luard to 'clear' his name.

No woman was ever named as Charles Luard's mistress.

No man was ever named as Caroline Luard's lover.

Charles and Caroline's surviving son, Captain Elmhurst Luard, was killed in France in September 1914, shortly after the outbreak of World War I.

Author's Note

Most of the characters in this story existed and are real. A few – the Blaines, the Farrells, Sarah Anderson and Amy Pegg – are my own invention.

1908 was a time of change in Britain. Herbert Asquith, the leader of the Liberal Party, was Prime Minister. Mrs Pankhurst was fighting for votes for women. And Europe was in the run-up to the most shocking and awful war the world had ever seen.

With the help of his Chancellor, David Lloyd George, Asquith laid the way for the Welfare State. The workhouses were closed, the poor were given access to education, and the Old Age Pension was introduced.

Such measures meant that wealthy women like Caroline Luard – who spent their days working on behalf of the poor – would no longer be needed. In future the State would decide how much benefit a person could receive, and these moves were already under way at the time of Caroline's death.

In view of the hate campaign against Charles afterwards, I think it probable that Caroline, too, was disliked by many of her neighbours. Few people enjoy taking charity, particularly if they have to beg for it. And if Caroline put conditions on the money she handed out, she would have made enemies.

I don't know if young men like Michael Blaine and Will Farrell lived in and around Ightham in 1908. But I find it easier to believe that Caroline was murdered by someone she knew rather than by a stranger.

Clearly many people thought the same at the time otherwise they wouldn't have focused the blame on her husband. But, apart from the Major-General, little attention was given to anyone else in the area. Police effort was put into searching for vagrants and finding witnesses to Charles Luard's alibi.

For myself, I have never believed that the

Major-General shot his wife or hired someone else to do it for him. His alibi depended entirely on chance. He could not have known that Thomas Durrand would be outside Hall Farm when he passed by, nor that a labourer would see him ten minutes later.

Had he been guilty, he would have stayed at the Golf Club as long as he could – acting normally, talking to friends, buying drinks – until the tragic news came through that someone else had found Caroline's body.

Instead, he collected his golf bag, spoke to no one, accepted a lift home from the vicar and put himself in the dangerous position of being the last person to see Caroline alive and the first to find her dead.

I believe Charles loved Caroline. And I believe what he wrote in his last letter to his friend.

'The dreadful murder of my wife has robbed me of all my happiness.'

For those interested in further research,
a factual retelling of the murder can
be found on Wikipedia.
http://en.wikipedia.org/wiki/Caroline_Mary_Luard

Books in the Quick Reads series

Amy's Diary	Maureen Lee
Beyond the Bounty	Tony Parsons
Bloody Valentine	James Patterson
Buster Fleabags	Rolf Harris
Chickenfeed	Minette Walters
Cleanskin	Val McDermid
The Cleverness of Ladies	Alexander McCall Smith
Clouded Vision	Linwood Barclay
A Cool Head	Ian Rankin
The Dare	John Boyne
Doctor Who: Code of the Krillitanes	Justin Richards
Doctor Who: Made of Steel	Terrance Dicks
Doctor Who: Magic of the Angels	Jacqueline Rayner
Doctor Who: Revenge of the Judoon	Terrance Dicks
Doctor Who: The Silurian Gift	Mike Tucker
Doctor Who: The Sontaran Games	Jacqueline Rayner
A Dreadful Murder	Minette Walters
A Dream Come True	Maureen Lee
Follow Me	Sheila O'Flanagan
Full House	Maeve Binchy
Get the Life You Really Want	James Caan
The Grey Man	Andy McNab
Hello Mum	Bernardine Evaristo

Start a new chapter

Quick Reads are brilliant short new books by bestselling authors and celebrities. We hope you enjoyed this one!

Find out more at **www.quickreads.org.uk**

🐦 @Quick_Reads   f Quick-Reads

We would like to thank all our funders:

LOTTERY FUNDED

We would also like to thank all our partners in the Quick Reads project for their help and support: NIACE, unionlearn, National Book Tokens, The Reading Agency, National Literacy Trust, Welsh Books Council, The Big Plus Scotland, DELNI, NALA

At Quick Reads, World Book Day and World Book Night we want to encourage everyone in the UK and Ireland to read more and discover the joy of books.

World Book Day is on 7 March 2013
Find out more at **www.worldbookday.com**

World Book Night is on 23 April 2013
Find out more at **www.worldbooknight.org**

Why not start a Quick Reads reading group?

If you have enjoyed this book, why not share your next Quick Read with friends, colleagues, or neighbours.

A reading group is a great way to get the most out of a book and is easy to arrange. All you need is a group of people, a place to meet and a date and time that works for everyone.

Use the first meeting to decide which book to read first and how the group will operate. Conversation doesn't have to stick rigidly to the book. Here are some suggested themes for discussions:

- How important was the plot?
- What messages are in the book?
- Discuss the characters – were they believable and could you relate to them?
- How important was the setting to the story?
- Are the themes timeless?
- Personal reactions – what did you like or not like about the book?

There is a free toolkit with lots of ideas to help you run a Quick Reads reading group at **www.quickreads.org.uk**

Share your experiences of your group on Twitter ✔ @Quick_Reads

For more ideas, offers and groups to join visit Reading Groups for Everyone at **www.readingagency.org.uk/readinggroups**

Enjoy this book?

Find out about all the others at **www.quickreads.org.uk**

For Quick Reads audio clips as well as videos
and ideas to help you enjoy reading visit
www.bbc.co.uk/skillswise

Join the Reading Agency's Six Book Challenge at
www.readingagency.org.uk/sixbookchallenge

Find more books for new readers at
www.newisland.ie
www.barringtonstoke.co.uk

Free courses to develop your skills are available in your
local area. To find out more phone 0800 100 900.

For more information on developing your skills
in Scotland visit **www.thebigplus.com**

Want to read more? Join your local library. You can borrow
books for free and take part in inspiring reading activities.